little Miss Tiny

by Roger Hargreaves

Little Miss Tiny was extremely small.

Not very tall at all!

She was so very tiny she didn't live in a house.

Do you know where she lived?

In a mousehole, in the dining room of
Home Farm.

She had made the mousehole quite comfortable really, and luckily there weren't any mice because the farm cat had chased them all away.

The trouble was, because she was so tiny, nobody knew she lived there.

Nobody had noticed her.

Not even the farmer and his wife.

So, there she lived.

All alone.

With nobody to talk to.

She was very lonely.

And sad.

Oh dear!

One day she was feeling so lonely she decided to be very brave and go for a walk.

Out of her mousehole she came.

She crept across the dining room and went through the crack in the door and into the hall.

To little Miss Tiny the hall looked as big as a field, and she scuttled across it to the back door of the farm.

Luckily for her the letterbox was at the bottom of the door and she squeezed herself through it and onto the doorstep.

It was all very exciting!

There before her was the farmyard.

She went exploring.

She came to a door with a gap at the bottom, and ducked in underneath.

There, inside, was a pig.

A large pig!

And, if you're as small as little Miss Tiny, a large pig looks very large indeed.

Miss Tiny looked at the pig.

The pig looked at Miss Tiny.

"Oink," he grunted, and moved closer to inspect this little person who had entered his sty.

"Oh my goodness me," squeaked little Miss Tiny in alarm, and shot out of the pigsty as fast as ever her little legs would carry her.

Which wasn't very fast because her legs were so very little!

She ran right around to the back of the pigsty before she stopped.

She leaned against the wall and put her hands over her eyes, and tried to get her breath back.

Suddenly, she heard a noise.

A very close noise.

A sort of breathing noise.

Very close indeed!

Oh!

She hardly dared take her hands away from her eyes, but when she did she wished she hadn't.

What do you think it was, there, right in front of her, looking at her with green eyes?

Ginger!

The farm cat!!

Poor little Miss Tiny.

Ginger grinned, showing his teeth.

"HELP!" shrieked Miss Tiny at the top of her voice.

"Oh somebody please HELP!"

The trouble was, the top of little Miss Tiny's voice was not a very loud place.

Ginger grinned another grin.

Every day Mr Strong went to Home Farm
to buy some eggs.

He liked eggs.

Lots of them.

That day he was walking home across the
farmyard when he heard a very tiny squeak.

He stopped.

There it was again.

Round the corner.

He looked round the corner and saw Ginger
and the poor trapped little Miss Tiny.

"SHOO!" said Mr Strong to Ginger, and picked up little Miss Tiny.

Very gently.

"Hello," he said. "Who are you?"

"I'm... I'm... I'm... Miss Tiny."

"You are, aren't you?" smiled Mr Strong.

"Well, if I was as tiny as you, I wouldn't go wandering around large farmyards!"

"But..." said Miss Tiny, and told Mr Strong about how she was so lonely she had to come out to find somebody to talk to.

"Oh dear," said Mr Strong. "Well now, let's see if we can't find you some friends to talk to."

And now, every week, Mr Strong collects little Miss Tiny and takes her off to see her friends.

Three weeks ago he took her to see Mr Funny, who told her so many jokes she just couldn't stop laughing all day.

Two weeks ago he took her to see Mr Greedy.

He told her his recipe for his favourite meal.

"But that's much much too much for tiny little me", she laughed.

Mr Greedy grinned.

"For you", he said, "divide by a hundred!"

Last week Mr Strong took her to see Mr Silly.

And Mr Silly showed her how to stand on your head.

"That's very silly," giggled little Miss Tiny.

"Thank you," replied Mr Silly, modestly.

And guess who she met this week?

Somebody who's become a special little friend.

"I never thought I'd ever meet anybody smaller than myself," laughed Mr Small.

Little Miss Tiny looked up at him, and smiled.

"You wait till I grow up," she said.

3 Great Offers for MR. MEN Fans!

MR. MEN TOKEN

1 New Mr. Men or Little Miss Library Bus Presentation Cases

A brand new stronger, roomier school bus library box, with sturdy carrying handle and stay-closed fasteners.

The full colour, wipe-clean boxes make a great home for your full collection.

They're just £5.99 inc P&P and free bookmark!

☐ MR. MEN ☐ LITTLE MISS (please tick and order overleaf)

PLEASE STICK YOUR 50P COIN HERE

2 Door Hangers and Posters

In every Mr. Men and Little Miss book like this one, you will find a special token. Collect 6 tokens and we will send you a brilliant Mr. Men or Little Miss poster and a Mr. Men or Little Miss double sided full colour bedroom door hanger of your choice. Simply tick your choice in the list and tape a 50p coin for your two items to this page.

Door Hangers (please tick)
☐ Mr. Nosey & Mr. Muddle
☐ Mr. Slow & Mr. Busy
☐ Mr. Messy & Mr. Quiet
☐ Mr. Perfect & Mr. Forgetful
☐ Little Miss Fun & Little Miss Late
☐ Little Miss Helpful & Little Miss Tidy
☐ Little Miss Busy & Little Miss Brainy
☐ Little Miss Star & Little Miss Fun

Posters (please tick)
☐ MR. MEN
☐ LITTLE MISS

3 Sixteen Beautiful Fridge Magnets – any 2 for £2.00!
inc.P&P

They're very special collector's items!
Simply tick your first and second* choices from the list below
of any 2 characters!

1st Choice
- ☐ Mr. Happy
- ☐ Mr. Lazy
- ☐ Mr. Topsy-Turvy
- ☐ Mr. Bounce
- ☐ Mr. Bump
- ☐ Mr. Small
- ☐ Mr. Snow
- ☐ Mr. Wrong

- ☐ Mr. Daydream
- ☐ Mr. Tickle
- ☐ Mr. Greedy
- ☐ Mr. Funny
- ☐ Little Miss Giggles
- ☐ Little Miss Splendid
- ☐ Little Miss Naughty
- ☐ Little Miss Sunshine

2nd Choice
- ☐ Mr. Happy
- ☐ Mr. Lazy
- ☐ Mr. Topsy-Turvy
- ☐ Mr. Bounce
- ☐ Mr. Bump
- ☐ Mr. Small
- ☐ Mr. Snow
- ☐ Mr. Wrong

- ☐ Mr. Daydream
- ☐ Mr. Tickle
- ☐ Mr. Greedy
- ☐ Mr. Funny
- ☐ Little Miss Giggles
- ☐ Little Miss Splendid
- ☐ Little Miss Naughty
- ☐ Little Miss Sunshine

*Only in case your first choice is out of stock.

CUT ALONG DOTTED LINE AND RETURN THIS WHOLE PAGE

--- **TO BE COMPLETED BY AN ADULT** ---

**To apply for any of these great offers, ask an adult to complete the coupon below and send it with
the appropriate payment and tokens, if needed, to MR. MEN OFFERS, PO BOX 7, MANCHESTER M19 2HD**

☐ Please send _____ Mr. Men Library case(s) and/or _____ Little Miss Library case(s) at £5.99 each inc P&P

☐ Please send a poster and door hanger as selected overleaf. I enclose six tokens plus a 50p coin for P&P

☐ Please send me _____ pair(s) of Mr. Men/Little Miss fridge magnets, as selected above at £2.00 inc P&P

Fan's Name _____

Address _____

_____ **Postcode** _____

Date of Birth _____

Name of Parent/Guardian _____

Total amount enclosed £ _____

☐ **I enclose a cheque/postal order payable to Egmont Books Limited**

☐ **Please charge my MasterCard/Visa/Amex/Switch or Delta account** (delete as appropriate)

| | | | | | | | | | | | | | | | | Card Number

Expiry date ___ / ___   **Signature** _____

Please allow 28 days for delivery. We reserve the right to change the terms of this offer at any time
but we offer a 14 day money back guarantee. This does not affect your statutory rights.

MR.MEN   **LITTLE MISS**
Mr. Men and Little Miss™ & ©Mrs. Roger Hargreaves.